Tiddler

Julia Donaldson & Axel Scheffler

ALISON GREEN BOOKS

D0715237

Once there was a fish and his name was Tiddler.
He wasn't much to look at, with his plain grey scales.
But Tiddler was a fish with a big imagination.
He blew small bubbles but he told tall tales.

"Sorry I'm late. I was riding on a seahorse."

"Sorry I'm late. I was flying with a ray."

"Sorry I'm late. I was diving with a dolphin."

Tiddler told a different story every day.

At nine o'clock on Monday,
Miss Skate called the register.
"Little Johnny Dory?"

"Yes, Miss Skate."

"Rabbitfish?" "Yes, Miss."

"Redfin?" "Yes, Miss."

"Tiddler? Tiddler?

TIDDLER'S LATE!"

"Sorry I'm late. I was swimming round a shipwreck.

I swam into a treasure chest, and someone closed the lid.

I bashed and I thrashed till a mermaid let me out again."

"Oh, no, she didn't." "OH, YES, SHE DID."

"It's only a story," said Rabbitfish and Redfin.   "Just a silly story," said Dragonfish and Dab.

"I *like* Tiddler's story,"
said Little Johnny Dory,

And he told it to his granny, who told it to a crab.

At nine o'clock on Tuesday, Miss Skate called the register.
"Little Johnny Dory?" "Yes, Miss Skate."
"Spiderfish?" "Yes, Miss." "Sunfish?" "Yes, Miss."
"Tiddler? Tiddler?

TIDDLER'S LATE!"

 "Sorry I'm late, Miss. I set off really early
But on the way to school I was captured by a squid.
I wriggled and I struggled till a turtle came and rescued me."
"Oh, no, he didn't." "OH, YES, HE DID."

"It's only a story," said Spiderfish and Sunfish.

"Just a silly story," said Devilfish and Dace.

"I *love* Tiddler's story,"
said Little Johnny Dory,

And he told it to his granny, who told it to a plaice . . .

Who told it to a starfish,

who told it to a seal,

Who told it to a lobster,

who told it to an eel . . .

At nine o'clock on Wednesday,
Tiddler was dawdling,
Dreaming up a story,
his tallest story yet.

Lost inside his story,
he didn't see the fishing boat.

He didn't hear the fishermen.
He didn't spot . . .

. . . the NET.

Meanwhile, in the schoolroom,
Miss Skate called the register.
"Little Johnny Dory?"

 "Yes, Miss Skate."

"Leopardfish?" "Yes, Miss."

 "Leaf Fish?" "Yes, Miss."

"Tiddler? Tiddler?

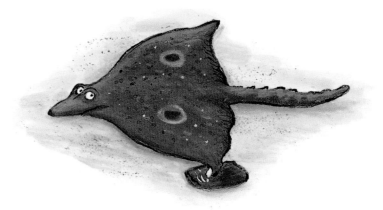

TIDDLER'S LATE!"

Ten o'clock . . .

eleven o'clock. Still no Tiddler!

Twelve o'clock, lunchtime.
Where could he be?

Far away, the fishermen were
hauling in their fishing net . . .

"This one's just a tiddler.
We'll throw it back to sea."

Tiddler was lost in the middle of the ocean
Where strange lights glimmered . . .

. . . and strange fish flew.

He swam around in circles.

He shivered in the seaweed.
But then he heard a story,
a story that he knew . . .

"Tiddler rode a seahorse.

Tiddler met a mermaid.

Tiddler met a turtle, who saved him from a squid.

Tiddler found a shipwreck.

Tiddler found a treasure chest."

"Oh, no, he didn't."

"OH, YES, HE DID."

Tiddler peeped out, and he saw a shoal of anchovies.

"Excuse me, can you tell me where you heard that tale?"

"We heard it from a shrimp,

but we don't know where *she* heard it."

And they took him to
the shrimp, who said,
"I heard it from a whale."

"I heard it from a herring."

"I heard it from an eel."

"I heard it from a lobster."

"I heard it from a seal."

"I heard it from a starfish."

"I heard it from a plaice."

The plaice said, "Just a minute, don't I recognise your face?"

"I'm Tiddler," said Tiddler.
"I'm tracking down my story."
The plaice replied, "I heard it from
my neighbour, Granny Dory."

One o'clock,   two o'clock . . . still no Tiddler.

Nearly hometime. Where could he be?
Just as the fishes were finishing their lessons . . .

IN SWAM TIDDLER
at half past three!

"Sorry I'm late but I swam into a fishing net.
I managed to escape, and I swam away and hid.
I was lost, I was scared, but
   a STORY led me home again."
"Oh, no, it didn't." "OH, YES, IT DID."

 "It's just another story," said
Leopardfish and Leaf Fish.

 "Just a silly story," said
Butterfish and Blue.

 "It isn't just a story," said
Little Johnny Dory . . .

And he told it to a writer friend . . .
who wrote it down for YOU.

For Luca – A.S.
For Liam and his dad at the Bermuda Aquarium – J.D.

First published in the UK in 2007 by
Alison Green Books
An imprint of Scholastic Children's Books
Euston House, 24 Eversholt Street
London NW1 1DB, UK
A division of Scholastic Ltd
www.scholastic.co.uk
London – New York – Toronto – Sydney – Auckland
Mexico City – New Delhi – Hong Kong
This paperback edition published 2016

PB ISBN: 978 1 407170 75 6

13 15 17 19 20 18 16 14 12